THIS BOOK BELONGS TO

· ·

Published by In The Making Publishing in the UK in 2021

Copyright © Tierney Collins 2021

Tierney Collins has asserted her right under
the Copyright, Designs and Patents Act, 1988,
to be identified as the author of this work.

Paperback ISBN 978-1-7399510-0-9

Illustrated by Reka Kadar

Typeset by SpiffingCovers.com

The Adventures of Percy - the - Pound

WRITTEN BY
Tierney Collins

ILLUSTRATED BY
Reka Kadar

Published by

In The Making
PUBLISHING

The morning began with
a startling sound,
an adventure awaited
for Percy the Pound.

The coins in Piggy the Bank
were all rattled awake,
as the place they called home
had started to shake.

Percy knew that noise too well
and let out a big sigh.
Shortly, a few friends of his
would have to say goodbye.

But this time was different.
It was now Percy's chance,
he was so excited to be picked
he just wanted to dance.

"Hi, my name is Penny and well... I'm only small. Tommy the Two Pound says I'm not worth much at all."

"You see, my friends and I have lived here for oh so many years. But pennies are never chosen," she said through floods of tears.

"Penny don't listen to bullies
Tommy is so wrong.
There wouldn't be us without you,
so, remember that you're strong."

Percy's first stop
was a shop full of sweets.
He waited next to Penny
as Leo picked out his treats.

Leo handed Percy to the lady who placed him in a till,
with many other coins all shiny sitting still.

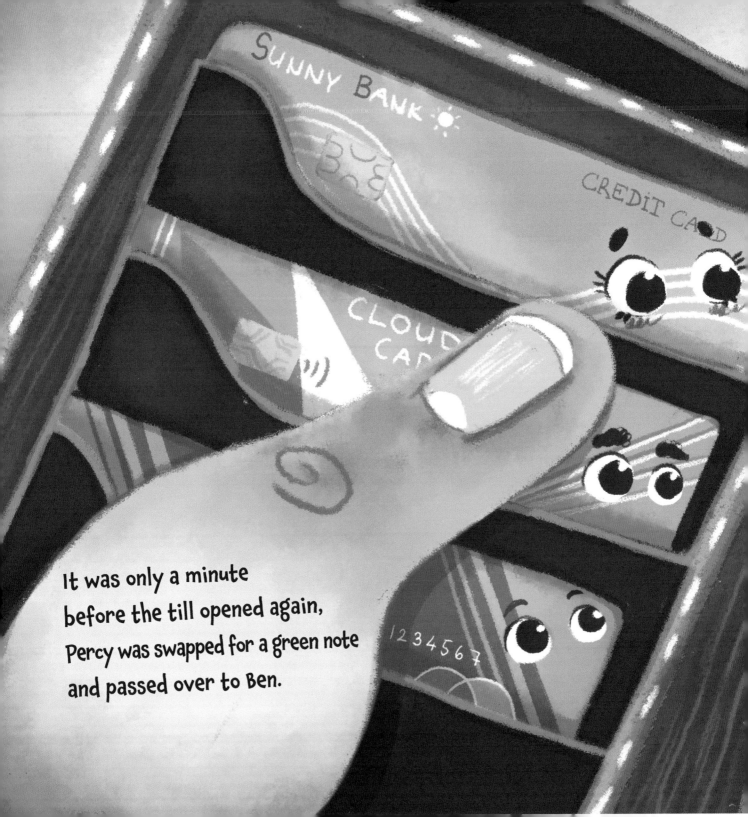

It was only a minute
before the till opened again,
Percy was swapped for a green note
and passed over to Ben.

"Hi, it's nice to meet you all,
I'm Percy the Pound."
Then a group of different coins
all stopped and turned around.

"Alright mate, I'm Quinny the Quid,
and how are you today?
I'm a pound like yourself,
and I come from London way."

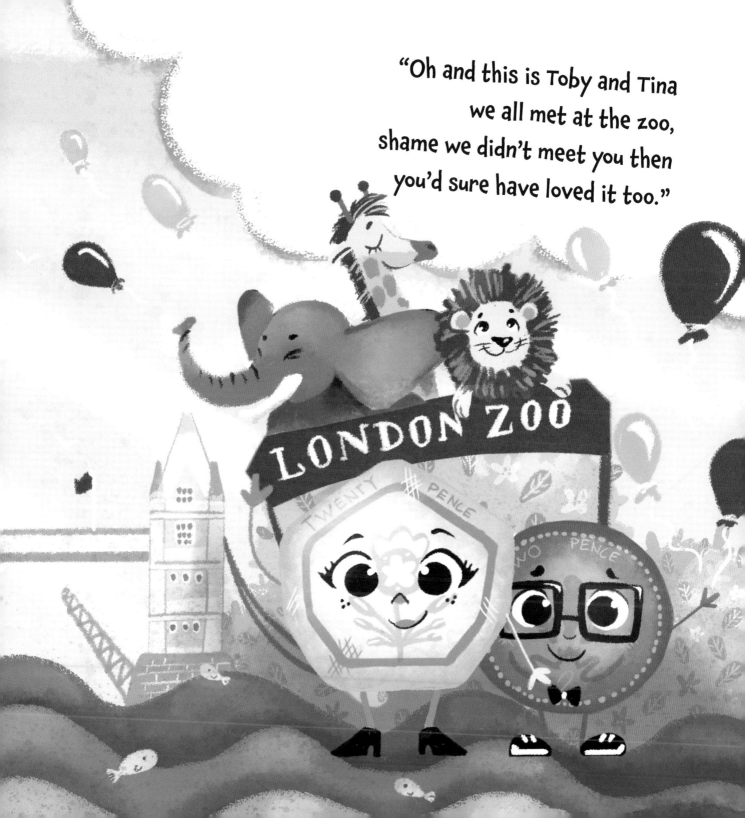

"Oh and this is Toby and Tina
we all met at the zoo,
shame we didn't meet you then
you'd sure have loved it too."

When it was Percy's time
to next see the light,
he was thrown in a case
to a musician's delight.

Percy enjoyed listening to the man
as he played song after song.
Together the coins and notes
all happily hummed along.

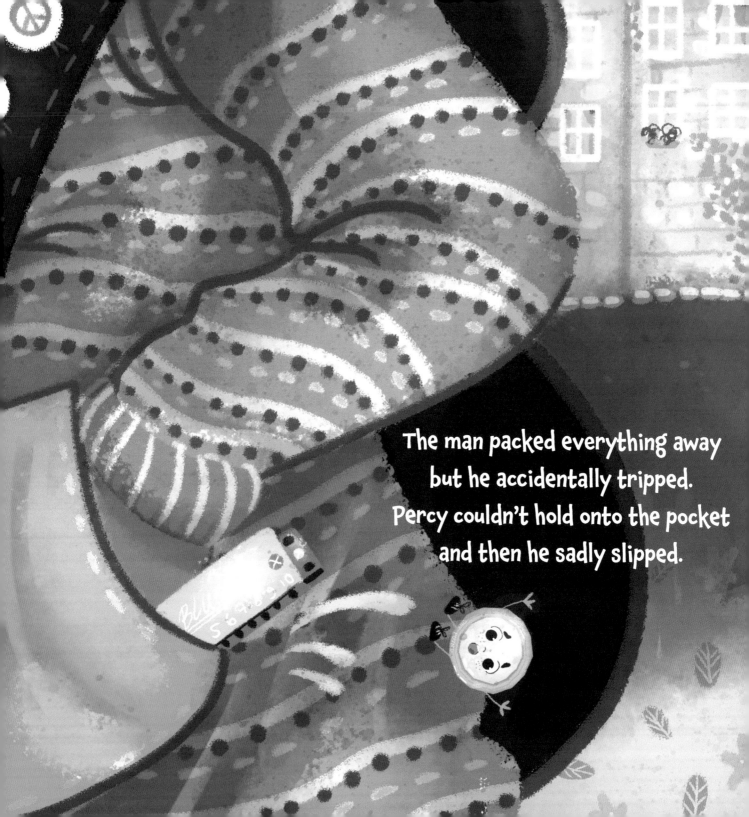

The man packed everything away
but he accidentally tripped.
Percy couldn't hold onto the pocket
and then he sadly slipped.

Tumbling and falling
all the way to the ground.

The concrete was the next stop
for poor Percy the Pound.

Percy was chilly and scared
and then it started to rain.
But suddenly a little girl
came skipping down the lane.

She chased after some litter
and threw it in the bin,
"That's better isn't it," she said
and gave Granny a grin.

"Wait, Granny over there," she yelled.
"Granny, do you see?
There's something round and sparkly,
right under that tree!"

"Dear girl, you've spotted a pound and what they say is true.
Be kind to the world and the world will be kind to you."

Printed in Great Britain
by Amazon